Gg
Hh
Ii
Jj
Kk
Ll
Mm
Uu
Vv
Ww
Xx
Yy
Zz

Dear Parent,

The My First Steps to Reading® *series is based on a teaching activity that helps children learn to recognize letters and their sounds. The use of predictable language patterns and repetition of familiar words will also help your child build a basic sight vocabulary. Your child will enjoy watching the characters in the books place imaginative objects in "letter boxes." You and your child can even create and fill your own letter box, using stuffed animals, cut-out pictures, or other objects beginning with the same letter. The things you can do together are limited only by your imagination. Learning letters will be fun—the first important step on the road to reading.*

The Editors

Published by Scholastic Inc., 90 Old Sherman Turnpike, Danbury, Connecticut 06810, by arrangement with The Child's World, Inc.

Originally published as *My "f" Sound Box* by The Child's World, Inc.

ISBN 0-7172-6505-6

Printed in the U.S.A.

My "f" Book

(Blends are included in this book.)

written by Jane Belk Moncure
illustrated by Colin King

Little f had a box.

"I will find things that begin with my 'f' sound," she said.

"I will put them into

my sound box."

Little f found a fishing rod.

She caught
four fish.

Did she put the
fishing rod and the
four fish into her box?

She did.

Then she caught five fat frogs.

Did she put the five fat frogs into the box with the fishing rod and the four fish? She did.

Little f walked through a forest of

fir trees.

She put a fir tree into her box.

“I will leave the other fir trees in the forest,” she said.

Suddenly, she saw a 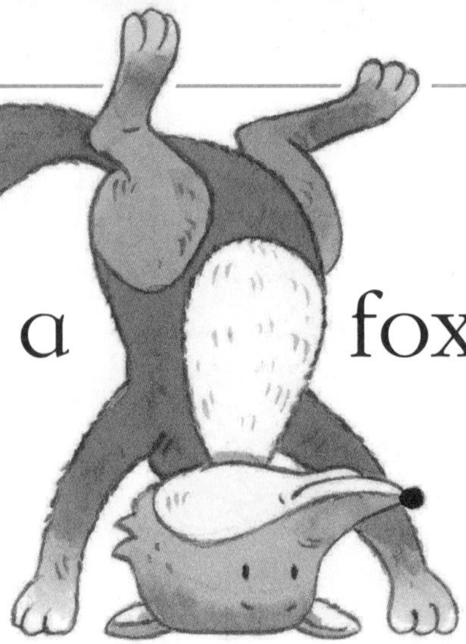 fox.
It was a funny fox!

"I will put this funny fox
into my box," said Little f.

"What funny things I have in my box!
I have a fishing rod,
four fish, five frogs,
a fir tree, and a fox!"

Little [f] came to a fence.

She climbed over the fence and saw . . .

a field of flowers.

She filled her box with flowers.

Then Little f saw a farmhouse.

The farmer ran from the farmhouse.

"Fire!" he cried.

"The farmhouse is on fire! Help!"

"Fire! Fire!" cried Little f.

She ran back through the field of flowers,

over the fence,

through the fir forest,

and all the way to the . . .

"Fire! Fire! Fire!" she shouted.
"The farmhouse is on fire!"

She rang the fire alarm.

Five firefighters jumped on a fire engine.

Little f wanted to help.

They gave Little f

a fire hose,

a firefighter's hat, boots,

and a firefighter's coat.

The fire engine went fast.

The firefighters put out the fire.

"Thank you," said the farmer.

"Thank Little f,"

said the five firefighters.
"She is our friend."

Then the firefighters took Little f and
her box back to the fire station.

Little f opened her box and took out the funny fox.
She played with all of her things.
fishing rod
four fish

My! What fun!
five fat frogs
flowers
fox
fir tree

Can you read these words
with Little
f
?
feet
fan
fork
flute

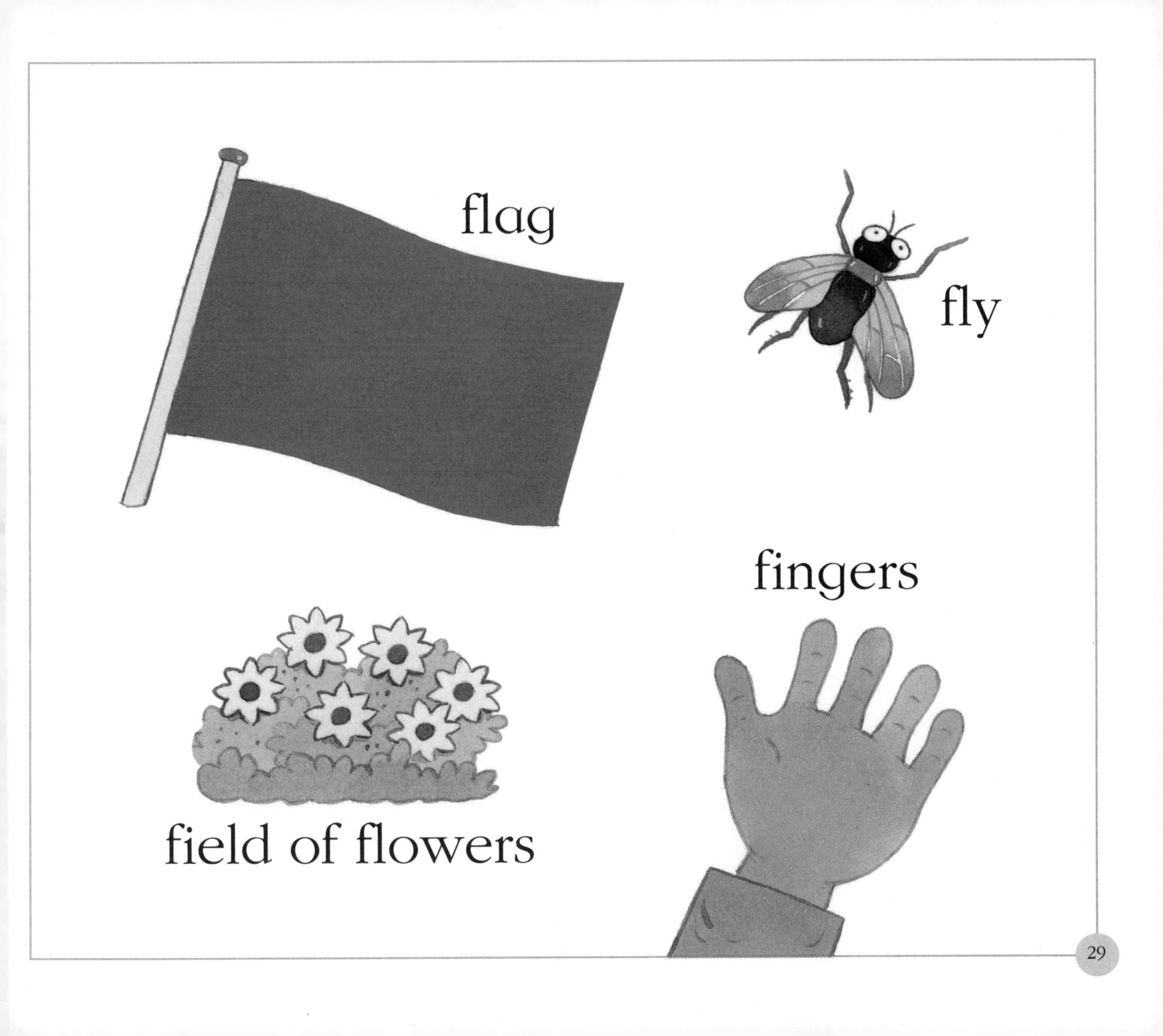
flag
fly
fingers
field of flowers

Aa
Bb
Cc
Dd
Ee
Ff
Nn
Oo
Pp
Qq
Rr
Ss
Tt
My First Steps to READING®